MW01379689

Tarantulas

Clint Twist

GARETH**STEVENS**
GS
PUBLISHING
A Member of the WRC Media Family of Companies

Please visit our web site at: www.garethstevens.com
For a free color catalog describing Gareth Stevens Publishing's list
of high-quality books and multimedia programs,
call 1-800-542-2595 (USA) or 1-800-387-3178 (Canada).
Gareth Stevens Publishing's fax: (414) 332-3567.

Library of Congress Cataloging-in-Publication Data

Twist, Clint.
    Tarantulas / Clint Twist. — North American ed.
        p. cm. — (Nature's minibeasts)
    Includes index.
    ISBN 0-8368-6377-1 (lib. bdg.)
    1. Tarantulas—Juvenile literature. I. Title.
QL458.42.T5T85   2006
595.4'4—dc22   2005054146

This North American edition first published in 2006 by
Gareth Stevens Publishing
A Member of the WRC Media Family of Companies
330 West Olive Street, Suite 100
Milwaukee, WI 53212 USA

Gareth Stevens series editor: Gini Holland
Gareth Stevens graphic designer: Dave Kowalski
Gareth Stevens art direction: Tammy West

Photo credits (t=top, b=bottom): Alamy: 8 (Danita Delimont), 15t (David Haynes), 17b (Jonathan Plant).
Getty Images: 6–7 (Digital Vision). FLPA: 2-3 (Mark Jones/Minden Pictures), 4–5 (Michael & Patricia Fogden/
Minden Pictures), 5 side panel, 9t, 12, 18, 19 side panel, 24b (Mark Moffett/Minden Pictures), 7t (Chris Mattison),
22 (Claus Meyer/Minden Pictures). OSF: 5, 13b (Nick Gordon), 21 side panel, 27t (Densey Clyne Productions).
Science Photo Library: 9 side panel, 13 side panel (Steve Gschmeissner), 11 side panel, 17 side panel, (Sinclair
Stammers), 15 side panel (Scott Camazine), 23 side panel (Andrew Syred).

Every effort has been made to trace the copyright holders for the photos in this book. The publisher apologizes
in advance for any unintentional omissions and would be pleased to insert appropriate acknowledgements in
any subsequent edition of this publication.

Printed in the United States of America

1 2 3 4 5 6 7 8 9 10 09 08 07 06

Words that appear in the glossary are printed in
boldface type the first time they occur in text.

Contents

What Are Tarantulas?

Tarantulas are spiders. Spiders are wingless, eight-legged **minibeasts**. They are not **insects**, because insects only have six legs. Tarantulas' legs can spread 12 inches (30 centimeters) apart. They are the largest spiders on Earth.

How do tarantulas live?

Like all spiders, tarantulas are **predators**. They are meat-eaters that hunt and kill other animals. Spiders mainly eat insects and other minibeasts, but tarantulas sometimes hunt much bigger **prey**, such as birds.

Tarantulas, like this red-kneed tarantula, are a big, hairy type of spider.

Tarantulas prefer to live in hot places such as South America and Africa.

UNDERSTANDING MINIBEASTS

Spiders belong to a group of minibeasts known as **arachnids.** Other kinds of arachnids are **scorpions**, ticks, and mites. Arachnids, like insects, are part of a larger group of minibeasts known as **arthropods**. An arthropod does not have an inner **skeleton** made of bones. Instead, it has tough outer skin, called an **exoskeleton**, that supports and protects its body.

Spiders, such as this tarantula, have to shed their exoskeletons in order to grow.

Where do tarantulas live?

Spiders are able to live anywhere except the North and South Poles, where it is too cold, and on the tops of the highest mountains. Tarantulas like to live in warm places like deserts and rain forests.

A Tarantula Up Close

A large tarantula 's body is about 2 inches (5 cm) across. Like all spiders, tarantulas have eight legs. Each leg can measure up to 4 inches (10 cm) in length.

All spiders have two parts to their bodies, the **prosoma** and the **abdomen**. The front part of the prosoma caries the spider's head with its eyes, strong **jaws**, sharp **fangs**, and its brain.

Toward the back of its prosoma, the spider has a pair of short **pedipalps**, or arms, that it uses to hold food close to its jaws. Behind its pedipalps, it has four pairs of walking legs.

legs

fangs

pedipalps

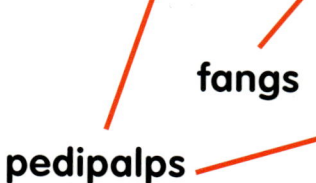

The narrowest part of a spider's body is in between its prosoma and its abdomen, as shown here on this red-rumped tarantula.

SPIDER SHAPE

The earliest spiders probably had three parts to their bodies, a head, a **thorax**, and an abdomen, just like insects. With spiders, the head and thorax gradually joined together into a single part, called the prosoma. With insects, however, the head and the thorax stayed separate.

abdomen

prosoma

Inside the abdomen, spiders have special **glands** that they use to produce **silk**. Tarantulas use silk to catch their prey and to line their nests.

The two main parts of a spider's body, the prosoma and the abdomen, are easy to spot in this pink tarantula.

Home Snug Home

Tarantulas live long lives. They live by themselves and do not form family groups. Females can live to be more than thirty-five years old, but males live only about half as long.

Tarantulas like to live in safe, dry, permanent nests. A tarantula may live in the same nest for all its adult life.

Some tarantulas like to live in holes in trees, but most prefer to live underground.

A tarantula digs its own burrow, which can reach as far as 30 inches (75 cm) under ground. Using its strong jaws, it can easily cut through even the hardest, sun-baked soil.

Tarantulas keep the opening to their burrows small to keep other creatures, and other big tarantulas like this one, from getting in.

A tarantula keeps its burrow as small as possible. It usually only has one place in its burrow where it has enough room to turn itself around.

This metallic pink toe tarantula has spun a silk lining to make its burrow soft and snug.

SILK PRODUCERS

Insects and spiders can both produce silk. With insects, only the **larvae,** or babies, produce silk. They spin a protective **cocoon** of silk around their soft bodies while growing. With spiders, however, the adults produce and spin silk. Some types of spiders use silk for building **webs,** and some spiders use silk to line their nests and to make **trip lines**.

A tarantula's prey is wrapped, and trapped, in silk.

Trip Lines

Most tarantulas spend much of their long lives hiding in their burrows and waiting for their prey to come along. After a big meal, a tarantula does not need to eat again for several weeks.

Some spiders spin webs to catch flying insects or to trap insects that crawl along the ground, but tarantulas do not. Although they do not spin webs, tarantulas use their silk in another way to catch their prey.

A tarantula will often spin a series of **trip lines** that spread out from its burrow like the spokes of a wheel.

Tarantulas, including this raft spider, attack prey with their fangs.

This tarantula settles down in its nest and waits for a minibeast or other animal to walk into the trip line.

One end of the line is attached to something solid, while the other end is attached to the tarantula's silken nest lining. Sitting in its nest, the tarantula can feel when its prey touches the line.

When it feels a tug on the line, a tarantula dashes out to kill its prey, just as this antilles pink toe does.

PARALYZING POISON

All spiders have **venom**, or poison, which is produced by special glands in their heads. Spiders inject venom into their victims through sharp, hollow fangs in their jaws. The venom paralyzes spider victims so they cannot move. Spiders want their prey to be alive when they eat them.

Tarantulas are all animal eaters. This one is eating a grasshopper.

Prowling for Prey

Some tarantulas do not like waiting for their prey, so they regularly go out and hunt. These include the largest, bird-eating tarantulas.

By day, however, tarantulas face danger when they go out of their burrows. Their large size makes them tempting targets for any spider-eating birds that may be flying above them.

Nighttime is much safer. After dark, the predator spider has less chance of becoming some other predator's prey.

Tarantulas are easy to spot in the daytime.

Tarantulas live mainly on a diet of large insects. The biggest tarantulas are able to attack small **mammals**, **lizards**, and even birds that are sitting on nests.

Larger tarantulas can eat animals as big as birds.

If a tarantula cannot find any large prey, it will collect lots of small insects. The spider will wrap them together with strands of silk and then eat them all at the same time.

A goliath bird-eating tarantula eats a snake.

LIQUID SILK

Spider silk starts out as a liquid produced by special glands inside the abdomen. The liquid squirts out of the spider's body through tiny holes at the base of the abdomen that are called **spinnerets**. The spider uses its legs to pull out the strands of liquid silk until they harden but remain sticky. Spider silk is much stronger than steel wire of the same thickness.

A tarantula's silk comes out of spinnerets such as this one.

Spider Senses

Some spiders have excellent eyesight. Others, including tarantulas, have very poor eyesight. All spiders, however, can feel vibrations, which is how they get information about their surroundings.

Tarantulas can feel tiny vibrations moving through each of their eight legs. Because their legs are spread out, they can also tell where the vibrations are coming from.

Most tarantulas have many weak eyes, such as these.

14

All spiders have hairs that feel vibration. Even spiders that do not look hairy have these hairs.

Tarantulas' hairs can pick up tiny vibrations.

Tarantulas have eight eyes at the fronts of their prosomas. Each eye can do little more than tell the difference between light and dark. Altogether, the eyes work just well enough to let the tarantula see movement.

Tarantulas, like this red kneed tarantula, use their leg hairs to find out about their surroundings.

ROWS OF EYES

Most spiders have eight eyes. Some have six or four, and some have only two. The eyes are usually arranged in two rows. Some spiders, such as jumping spiders, have two hunting eyes that can take in clear images. Most spiders, however, are like the tarantula. They have to live with poor eyesight.

Tarantulas' eyes always come in pairs. This jumping spider has one pair of large eyes and one pair of small eyes.

Striking Jaws

Scientists put spiders into two main groups, according to how spiders' jaws work. Tarantulas belong to the group that has jaws that strike downward.

fangs

A tarantula's fangs are on the front of its prosoma.

Tarantulas have two sharp fangs that they can bring down either together or one after the other, again and again, until their victims stop moving.

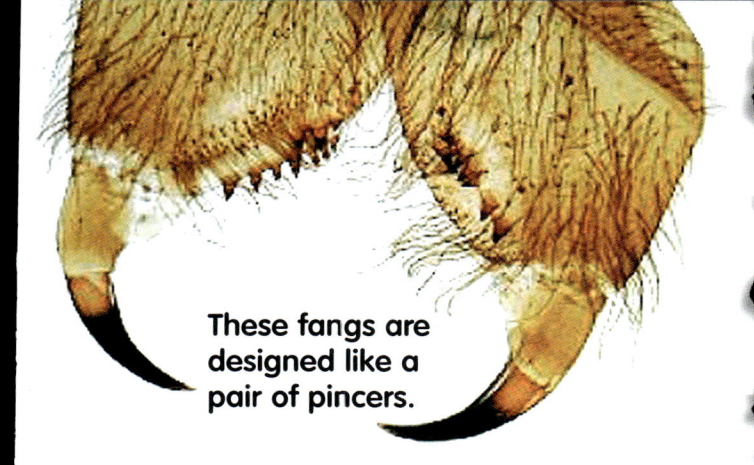

These fangs are designed like a pair of pincers.

The other group of spiders have jaws made to strike inward. They bring their fangs together so that the fangs meet like a pair of pincers. These fangs work better than downward striking jaws because they keep the victim from escaping.

Fangs

The fangs of this Chile rose tarantula are large and sharp enough to cut even the toughest insect exoskeleton.

LIQUEFIED FOOD

Spiders do not chew and crunch their food. They just slurp it up. Once its prey stops moving, the spider dribbles digestive juices into the wound made by its jaws. These juices turn the prey's insides into thick liquid goo that the spider sucks and slurps into its mouth. After a spider has finished eating, all that it leaves behind are tiny, dried up pieces that the spider cannot eat.

A crab spider sinks its fangs into a honeybee.

Search for a Mate

Tarantulas grow very slowly. They are not able to **mate** until they are about ten years old. Mating usually takes place during the hottest and driest parts of the year.

Male and female tarantulas live separately. They do not have many ways they can communicate to find each other. Instead, to find a mate, a tarantula must go out and hope that it bumps into another tarantula.

A female tarantula feels her trip lines shake. In this way, she senses that a male tarantula is outside her nest.

A salmon bird-eating tarantula defends itself.

Mating can be a risky business for males because female tarantulas usually prefer eating to mating. Because tarantulas are **cannibals**, mating males face real danger.

The male has to lift the female up in order to mate, just like this pampas gold tarantula is doing.

After mating, the male must run away quickly, or the female may decide the male is a tasty snack!

SAFETY SOUND

Spiders can make sound in a number of ways, such as by rubbing their legs together or drumming their legs on the ground. Many spiders use these sounds for simple communication. Males that are looking for a mate make a special safety sound as they move. If they make this sound, they are less likely to be attacked and eaten by a female.

The male jumping spider comes close to the female very carefully.

Spiderlings

Female tarantulas lay up to one thousand eggs at a time. Each egg is very small. The female holds the eggs together with strands of silk to make what is called an egg sac.

This ball of silk and eggs is about half the size of the female's body. The sticky silk prevents any of the eggs from falling or being lost.

The female usually just leaves the egg sac in the deepest part of her burrow and does not give her eggs any special care. If it rains and the burrow floods, however, the female will carry the egg sac to safety.

A female wolf spider carries her egg sac.

The eggs hatch into tiny **spiderlings.** Spiderlings look just like adult spiders, except they are tiny and almost colorless.

Little spiderlings hatch and crawl out of the egg sac.

Pet tarantulas can be born and raised in captivity.

Spiderlings can feed on tiny minibeasts in the soil that are much too small to fill up an adult tarantula.

SPIDER DEVELOPMENT

A spider's exoskeleton is not stretchy. It does not stretch as the spiderling grows in size. Instead, a growing spiderling grows a new, larger exoskeleton under its old, outgrown one. When its new exoskeleton is ready, its old one splits open and is left behind like a worn-out coat. Shedding the exoskeleton is known as **molting**.

Tarantulas molt several times before they are fully grown.

Tarantulas and Humans

The spiders we call tarantulas, even the biggest, are not usually deadly for human beings. Their bite can be painful, but the venom of tarantulas is too weak to have much effect except on people who are allergic to the venom.

The name tarantula first belonged to a much smaller spider, the European wolf spider. It was first named tarantula after the town of Taranto in Southern Italy, which is one of the places it lives. This spider was once thought to be very dangerous. It can give a painful bite, but it is not really dangerous.

The name tarantula has now been given to the hairy spiders of the world, such as this bird-eating tarantula.

A European wolf spider is the original tarantula spider.

Tarantulas often scare people because they are well known for their painful, poisonous bites. Many people are naturally afraid of spiders. Tarantulas are especially frightening because they are so big, and they do not just wait, but hunt, for their prey.

Wolf spiders like this one are not as dangerous as people once thought.

ITCHY HAIRS

In addition to their sharp fangs and poisonous venom, tarantulas have weapons hidden in their hairy covering. Some hairs are coated with poison and have sharp, fragile tips that easily break off. The poison on the hairs is not strong enough to harm a person, but if the tips become stuck in a person's skin, they can cause a very bad rash.

Tarantulas' hairs look like this when they are magnified.

Other Spiders

There are more than forty thousand different species of spiders. They all have two parts to their bodies and eight legs, but some spiders look very different from others.

Jumping Spiders

This group is one of the largest of the spider groups. All jumping spiders have two pairs of eyes, and they have very good eyesight. They jump on their prey, which can be up to 10 inches (25 cm) away, to catch it.

Jumping spiders have two pairs of eyes.

Curved Spiny Spiders

Some small spiders have spines and horns that give them an unusual look. Scientists believe that the spiders developed these horns and spines because this makes them difficult for birds to swallow and in that way helps them survive.

Flower Spiders

These spiders are also called crab spiders because they often walk sideways, the way crabs do. They wait on flowers to catch visiting insects. Some flower spiders can hide by changing the color of their bodies so they match the flowers they are sitting on.

Black Widows

Most people recognize the famous black widow spider with its red marks. This small creature has fangs that deliver very poisonous venom. The bite of a black widow is very painful, and the venom is strong enough to kill children and old people.

Spider Behavior

Many spiders live and hunt in much the same way as tarantulas. Others have different ways of life and very different ways of using their silk.

Web Spinners

The most well-known spiders are those that spin webs between branches to catch flying insects. This kind of spider sits at one corner of its web and waits to feel vibrations made by any insect that gets tangled up in the silk.

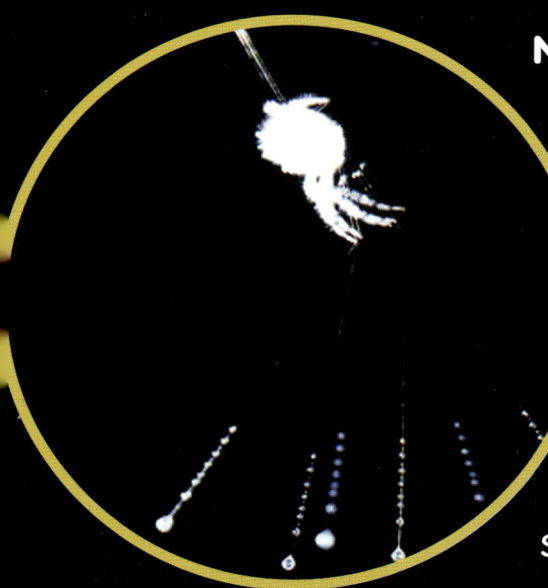

Net-Throwing Spiders

These spiders do not bother spinning a big web fixed in one place. Instead, they spin small webs like pieces of fishing nets. Each spider then holds this net between its two front pairs of legs and waits patiently on a branch. When an insect comes within reach, the spider drops its net to catch its victim.

Water Spiders

This spider is only found in fresh water. It spins a very thick web of silk and then traps bubbles of air in the web. The air in the bubbles lets the spider breathe underwater while it waits for prey, such as **tadpoles** and baby fish.

Spitting Spiders

Spitting spiders have special venom-filled silk glands that allow them to spit two streams of poisonous silk. They attack their insect prey by covering their victims with a zigzag pattern of threads, so the prey cannot fly away.

Life Cycle

After mating with a male, the female tarantula produces an egg sac made of silk that can contain up to one thousand tiny eggs. She puts the sac in a nest. Tiny spiderlings hatch from the eggs, crawl out of the egg sac, and come out of the nest after a few weeks. They care for themselves and grow into adult tarantulas that will then find mates to produce more eggs.

eggs

spiderlings

adult

Fabulous Facts

Fact 1: Tarantulas can be anywhere in size from as small as a fingernail to as big as a dinner plate.

Fact 2: For most people, tarantula bites are no worse than a bee sting.

Fact 3: Like cats, tarantulas have claws they can pull in.

Fact 4: As it grows into a full adult, a tarantula spiderling will molt about ten times.

Fact 5: Fear of spiders is called **arachnophobia**. It is one of the most common fears among humans.

Fact 6: Some tarantulas, who live in caves, have no eyes at all.

Fact 7: Tarantulas can be kept as house pets in a **terrarium.**

Fact 8: Female tarantulas usually live twenty to thirty years, but males live only ten to twelve years.

Fact 9: The fangs of most tarantulas are bigger than the fangs of most poisonous snakes, so their bites can make big cuts in their victims.

Fact 10: More than eight hundred different species of tarantulas have been found.

Fact 11: When threatened, some tarantulas make loud hissing noises by rubbing the bristles on their legs together.

Fact 12: One enemy of the tarantula is a large wasp called the tarantula hawk. It injects a tarantula with venom that paralyzes the tarantula. The wasp then lays an egg inside the paralyzed spider's body. The new wasp hatches and eats the tarantula alive!

Fact 13: People are one of the tarantula's greatest enemies, because they destroy so much of its habitat.

Glossary

abdomen — the largest part of a spider's two-part body, which holds most of its important organs

arachnids — a group of minibeasts that have a two-part body, the front part of which holds four pairs of legs but no antennae. This group includes spiders, scorpions, ticks, and mites.

arachnophobia — the fear of spiders

arthropods — minibeasts that have jointed legs, including insects and spiders

cannibals — animals that eat their own kind, such as tarantulas and some other spiders

cocoon — a protective covering of silk produced by insect larvae to protect their bodies while they change into adults

exoskeleton — a hard outer covering that supports and protects the bodies of many minibeasts

fangs — long sharp teeth, some of which are made to inject venom

glands — parts of an animal's body that are used to make particular substances, such as silk

insects — minibeasts with six jointed legs, three-part bodies, and usually also one or two pairs of wings

jaws — hinged structures around the mouth that help most animals bite and chew

larva/larvae — the form of certain young insects, such as bees, after they hatch from eggs. More than one larva are called larvae.

lizards — a group of mainly small to medium-sized reptiles

mammals — a group of warm-blooded animals that have an inner skeleton and that feed their young on milk

mate — to join adult bodies to produce babies

minibeasts — any of a large number of small land animals that do not have skeletons in their bodies

molting — the shedding of an insect or spider's exoskeleton so that it can grow

pedipalps — short, leg-like body parts that spiders use to hold food

predators — animals that hunt and eat other animals

prey — an animal that is eaten by another animal

prosoma — the front part of a spider's body, which is the head and the thorax joined together into a single body part

scorpions — minibeasts related to spiders that have long, flexible tails with venomous stings

silk — a natural thread produced by insect larvae and adult spiders

skeleton — an inner structure of bones that supports the body of an animal

spiderlings — any young spiders that are not yet fully grown

spinnerets — tiny holes, or nozzels, on a spider's abdomen that are used to squirt out silk

tadpoles — the young forms of frogs or toads, which do not look like the adults at first, but gradually take on adult body shapes

terrarium — a container to keep plants and animals

thorax — the middle part of an insect's body, to which the legs are attached

trip lines — silk strings that some spiders, especially tarantulas, stretch out to trip and trap their prey

venom — a poison produced by an animal for use against other animals, either to paralyze them or to kill them

webs — a net of silk threads that many spiders make to catch insects

Index